The Story of the Nativity

The Story of the Nativity

By Elizabeth Winthrop
Illustrated by Ruth Sanderson

Designed by Sylvia Frezzolini

Manufactured in the United States of America.

10 9 8 7 6 5 4 3 2 1

ISBN: 0-671-63019-9

Long ago in the land of Galilee, a carpenter named Joseph lived with his wife, Mary. Mary was going to have a baby.

One day, Mary and Joseph learned that they had to travel to the little town of Bethlehem, where Joseph had been born. Mary rode on their donkey's back. It was a long trip.

When they finally reached Bethlehem, it was
nighttime. The inn was already full of people.

"Can we stay here?" Joseph asked.

"We have no room," the innkeeper said.

"But we have traveled a long way and we are
very tired," said Joseph.

"You can stay in the back with the animals,"
said the innkeeper.

So Mary and Joseph spent the night in the
stable behind the inn.

The straw made a soft bed for them.

The animals gathered around
to keep them warm.

That night, the baby Jesus was born.

Mary wrapped the baby in swaddling clothes and laid him in the manger. Mary and Joseph gazed down in wonder at the newborn baby.

High above the little town of Bethlehem, the stars shone more brightly in the sky.

Even the animals knew something special had happened in their stable that night.

In the fields nearby, shepherds were watching over
their sheep.
Suddenly, an angel appeared in the sky above them.
The shepherds drew back in fear.

"Do not be afraid, for I bring you great news for all people," the angel said. "The Saviour has been born today in Bethlehem. You will find Him lying in a manger."

Soon a whole chorus of angels filled the sky. They sang songs to praise the newborn baby.

"Let us go to Bethlehem and find the baby," the shepherds said to each other. So they gathered their flocks together and went to worship the baby Jesus.

When the shepherds found Mary, Joseph, and
the baby in the stable, they, too knelt down to
worship Him.

After several days had passed, three wise men
from the East followed a star that led them to
the baby Jesus.

When the star came to rest over the stable in
Bethlehem, they knew that their long journey
was at an end.

The wise men found the baby with Mary and Joseph.
They knelt down and offered him their presents of gold
and frankincense and myrrh.

The baby that was born in Bethlehem would grow up
to be a great King. Even as he lay in the quiet darkness
of the stable, angels in Heaven were praising Him with
songs of "Glory to God in the highest."